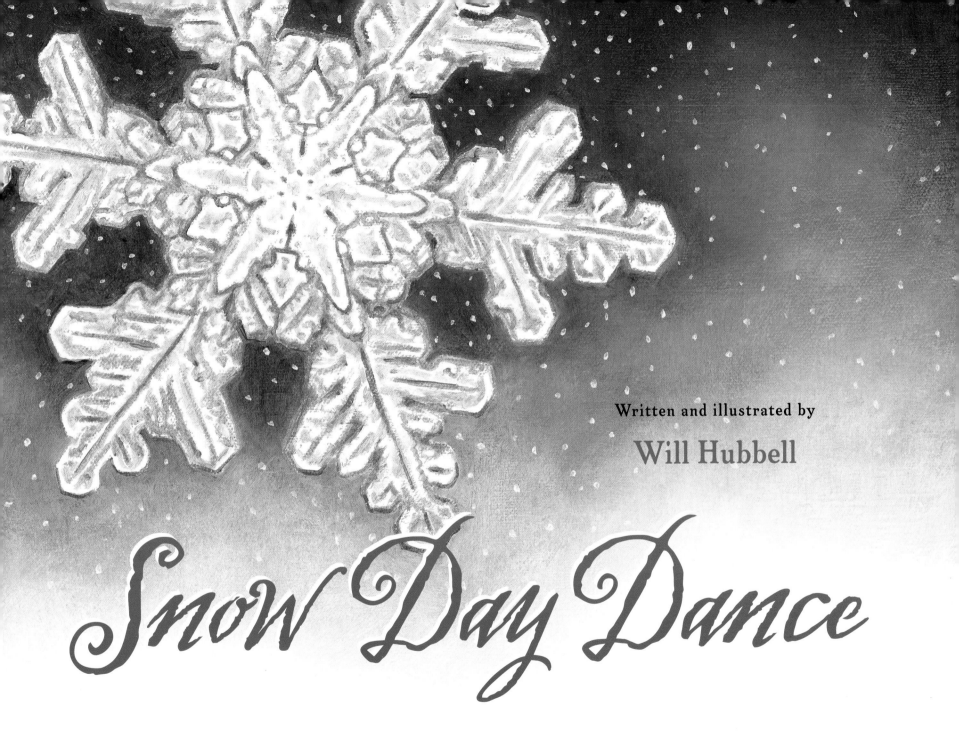

Written and illustrated by

Will Hubbell

Snow Day Dance

ALBERT WHITMAN & COMPANY, MORTON GROVE, ILLINOIS

High above our school, dark clouds fill the sky.
Inside the clouds, snowflakes grow until they're too heavy to float.
Then they fall.

We make paper snowflakes for the windows.

"Snowflakes have six sides," says our teacher, "and every flake is different."

We look outside. Our teacher does, too. Real snowflakes are beginning to cover everything.

With a sly smile, our teacher says, "Wear your pajamas backward tonight and do the magic dance."

"Why?" whispers the kid from a place with green winters.

"So we'll have a . . ."

"Shhh!" goes someone. "It won't happen if you say it."

So we say nothing, but we all think—*snow day!*

We walk home in flake-filled air. Cars whine and slip. Walking is faster.

Night comes, and the snow is still falling. Each streetlight has a
snowflake halo. Wearing our pajamas backward, we do the snow day dance.
In the morning, the radio says, "All schools closed."
We bounce with joy. A surprise vacation. A day for fun. A gift.

We go outside. Falling flakes soften every sound. Each snowflake looks like a tiny work of art. Together, in countless trillions, they change everything around us.

Cars hide under snowy quilts.

Fence posts wear hats. Snow snakes lie on the rails.

Trees are made of lace.

Walking is hard work. Each step squeaks and
leaves a hole. We get our sleds and head for the hill.

To a white and gray world, we bring color. Green and
purple sleds. Blue coats. Rosy cheeks.

Shoosh we go. Whee! Snowflakes lick our faces. Dogs, too.

All around us, snowflakes swirl like smoke, like dancing stars.

The woods fade, then disappear—hidden by the falling snow.

We feel alone until we see a shape. A rainbow polar bear?

No—our teacher, doing the snow day dance!

About Snow and Snowflakes

Snow begins with cold temperatures and clouds. When the temperature drops to 32º Fahrenheit (0º Celsius) or colder, the water droplets in clouds freeze and begin to form snow. The water clings to tiny dust particles; each particle is called an **ice nucleus** and it helps the molecules join together as they freeze. Water droplets are very small and light, so for snow to fall, the frozen droplets in a cloud must grow larger. They do this one molecule at a time, until eventually they become too heavy to float, and they tumble to earth.

Column

What we call snowflakes are really snow crystals. Crystals are made of identical molecules fitting together in a pattern. Since frozen water molecules make a hexagonal, or six-sided, pattern, snow crystals have six sides, too. Though the pattern is simple, snow crystals can have a variety of shapes. In fact, scientists who study snow crystals classify them into eighty different types!

The beautiful crystals we tend to think of as "snowflakes" are **stellar dendrites.** Other kinds of crystals are actually more common, such as hollow, six-sided **columns**—the same shape as a pencil—as well as **needles** and hexagonal **plates. Capped columns** are columns with a plate at each end. When snow crystals form inside clouds, the air temperature and moisture determine what types of crystals are made.

During a snowstorm, changes in the air usually create many kinds of crystals, and the shape and features of each snow crystal can tell us just how cold and wet it was inside the cloud at the moment the crystal

Stellar dendrite

Capped column

formed. It takes a lot of water vapor and very cold air (5º Fahrenheit, -15º Celsius) to make the fanciest and largest snow crystals, stellar dendrites. They begin as small, flat hexagons, which grow larger as water molecules in the air hit them and become part of their pattern. The molecules tend to attach themselves to the points of the hexagons until they stick out to form six branches. As more molecules attach to each branch, they form little branches of their own, giving the flake a beautiful, lacy appearance.

The conditions around the other snow crystals within the cloud are slightly different, which causes them to grow differently. That is why no two snowflakes are alike.

Stellar dendrites have six branches, but sometimes two plate crystal formations join together to make rare twelve-branched snowflakes.

Eighteen-sided and even twenty-four-sided flakes have been found, too!

As snow crystals fall, they may change further. Sometimes, they clump together to form fluffy balls. They may melt and refreeze into ice pellets. Strong updrafts can turn them into soft, irregular ice particles called graupel.

Two things are needed to make a snowstorm: lots of water vapor and cold temperatures to turn it into snow crystals. Great masses of moving air bring these two ingredients together. In the United States, a major winter storm often begins when cold and dry air from Canada and warm and wet air from the Gulf of Mexico meet. The collision of these two forces drives the storm and allows it to make plenty of snow crystals—sometimes, even enough to cause a snow day.

Needles and plate

To Carol, who taught me the dance.

Library of Congress Cataloging-in-Publication Data

Hubbell, Will.
Snow day dance / written and illustrated by Will Hubbell.
p. cm.
Summary: With their teacher's help, schoolchildren anticipate the
first snow of the season and enjoy their day off from school.
ISBN 0-8075-7523-2 (hardcover)
[1. Snow—Fiction. 2. Schools—Fiction. 3. Teachers—Fiction.] I. Title.
PZ7.H86312Sno 2005 [E]—dc22 2005003894

The artwork for this book was rendered in heat-set oil paints on canvas.
The design is by Will Hubbell and Carol Gildar.

For more information about Albert Whitman & Company, visit our web site at www.albertwhitman.com.